For Amelia

First published 1985 by
Walker Books Ltd
184-192 Drummond Street
London NW1 3HP

© 1985 Niki Daly

First printed 1985
Printed and bound by
L.E.G.O., Vicenza, Italy

British Library Cataloguing in Publication Data
Daly, Niki
Teddy's ear.–(Storytime; 1)
1. Readers–1950–
I. Title   II. Series
428.6   PE1119

ISBN 0-7445-0267-5

TEDDY'S EAR

Niki Daly

WALKER BOOKS
LONDON

Tim looked unhappy.

'What's the matter, Tim?' asked Mum.

'Look, Teddy's ear has come off,' said Tim.

'Don't worry,' said Mum. 'Maybe we can fix it.'

Mum took out her work-basket.
'Bring Teddy,' she said.

Mum got out a needle and some thread.

'What colour shall we use?' she asked.

Tim handed her the red thread.

'Be careful of the needle,' Mum said.

Mum sewed Teddy's ear back on.
'Here,' said Mum. 'Teddy's better now.'

So Tim held Teddy by the ear and took him for a walk.

Tim held Teddy by his ears and
gave him a swing.

He danced with Teddy.

He sang for Teddy.
'I lost my locket,
I lost my key,
I threw my Teddy
Right over the sea.'

Tim picked up Teddy and hugged him.

Teddy's ear was still on!